W9-BIR-748
Fuzzies
Fuzzies
Fuzzies
Fuzzies
Fuzzies

John Steven Gurney

PAPERCUTZ
New York

MORE GREAT GRAPHIC NOVEL SERIES AVAILABLE FROM

PAPERCUTZ™

THE SMURFS TALES

BRINA THE CAT

CAT & CAT

THE SISTERS

ATTACK OF THE STUFF

LOLA'S SUPER CLUB

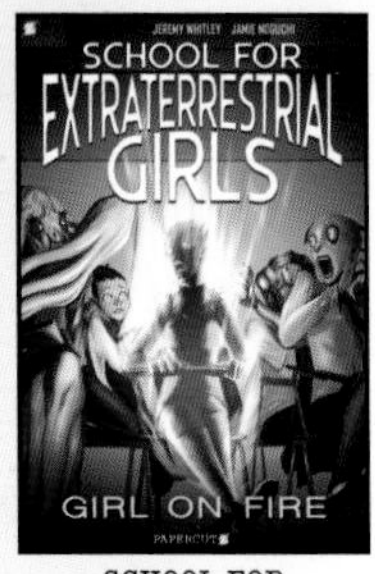

SCHOOL FOR EXTRATERRESTRIAL GIRLS

GERONIMO STILTON REPORTER

THE MYTHICS

GUMBY

MELOWY

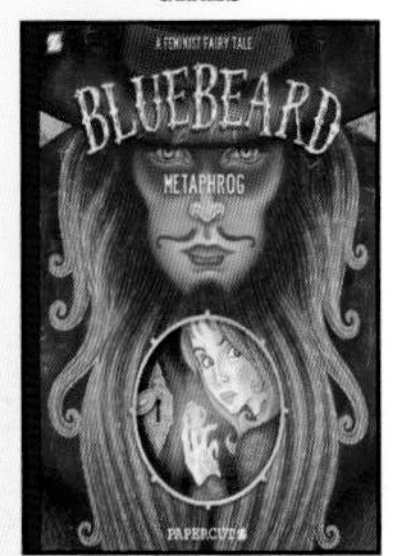

BLUEBEARD

GILLBERT

ASTERIX

FUZZY BASEBALL

THE CASAGRANDES

THE LOUD HOUSE

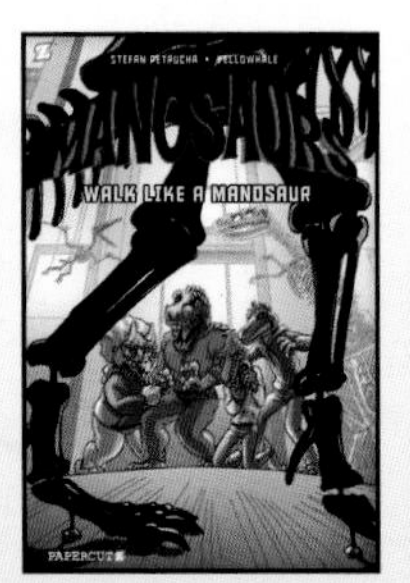

MANOSAURS

GEEKY F@B 5

THE ONLY LIVING GIRL

papercutz.com

Also available where ebooks are sold.

To Brattleboro Little League coach and math teacher David Cyr. And, to Kathie.

Fuzzy Baseball #4
"Di-No Hitters"

Created by JOHN STEVEN GURNEY

JAYJAY JACKSON—Production

JEFF WHITMAN—Managing Editor

JIM SALICRUP
Editor-in-Chief

Hardcover ISBN: 978-1-5458-0715-6

Paperback ISBN: 978-1-5458-0716-3

Printed in China
June 2021

Papercutz books may be purchased for business or promotional use.
For information on bulk purchases please contact Macmillan Corporate and Premium Sales Department at (800) 221-7945 x5442.

Distributed by Macmillan
First printing

THE TRIASSIC PARK TITANS

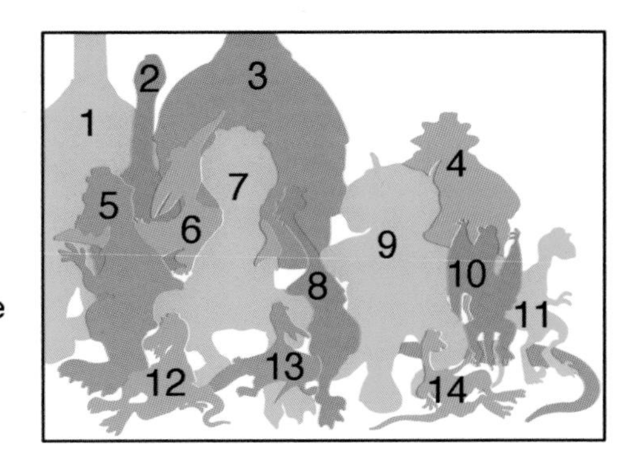

#1 Diplo Docus, Third Base
#2 Cam Arasorrus, First Base
#3 Brachio Zarus, Second Base
#4 Annie Kylo, Catcher
#5 Bump Rokhedd, Pitcher

#6 Terry Dactyl, Center Field
#7 Tyrell Rex, Pitcher
#8 Struthie O'Mimus, Shortstop
#9 Cap'n Spike Topps, Manager
#10 Donna Pterra, Left Field
#11 Vinny Rapto, First Base
#12 Masia K. Saurus, Second Base
#13 Ramfo Rinkus, Right Field
#14 Compo Nathus, Third Base

THE FERNWOOD VALLEY FUZZIES

#1/8 Blossom Honey-Possum, Centerfield
#7 Percivale Penguino, Right Field
#8 Pam the Lamb, Left Field
#10 Larry Boa, Third Base
#13 Pepe Perrito, Shortstop
#19 Kazuki Koala, Right Field
#21 Hammy Sosa, Catcher
#24 Pony Perez, Shortstop
#29 Red Kowasaki, Pitcher
#32 Sandy Kofox, Pitcher
#34 Bo Grizzly, First Base & Manager
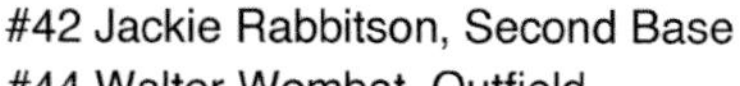
#42 Jackie Rabbitson, Second Base
#44 Walter Wombat, Outfield
#45 Kit Ocelot, Pitcher

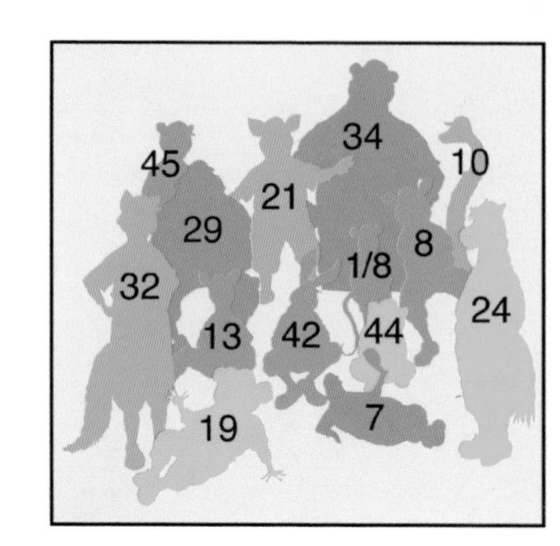

TALKIN' 'BOUT BOOKS
with
PROFESSOR RUFUS DeTERRIER

TODAY WE ARE CHATTING WITH JOHN STEVEN GURNEY ABOUT HIS FOURTH FUZZY BASEBALL BOOK, DI-NO HITTERS.
I'M PLEASED TO BE HERE PROFESSOR. I'M HOPING THIS BOOK WILL BE A HOME RUN WITH THE READERS!
DI-NO HITTERS

IT LOOKS LIKE THE FUZZIES ARE PLAYING A TEAM OF DINOSAURS THIS TIME AROUND. GREAT FUN!
THAT'S RIGHT, THE TRIASSIC PARK TITANS.
BUT ARE ANY OF THESE DINOSAURS EVEN FROM THE TRIASSIC PERIOD? I SEE SOME THAT ARE FROM THE JURASSIC, AND OTHERS FROM THE EARLY CRETACEOUS...
CHANNEL CHANGING DEVICE

YOU DO KNOW THIS BOOK IS FICTION, RIGHT? IT'S A COMEDY. THIS IS NOT A FACTUAL BOOK ABOUT DINOSAURS.
HEY, SPORTS FANS! *IZZY LIZARDO* HERE. WELCOME TO FUZZY FIELD! TODAY THE FUZZIES TAKE ON THE TRIASSIC PARK TITANS!

INTRODUCING THE TRIASSIC PARK TITANS!
KOFOX
32
1/8

GRIZZL
34
RABBITSO
42

GRIZ, HAVE YOU EVER PLAYED AGAINST PLAYERS THAT BIG?
IT'S NOT THE SIZE OF THE PLAYER THAT COUNTS.
Fuzzies
SOME OF THOSE DINOSAURS ARE SO BIG THAT THE BALL IS AS TINY AS A PEA TO THEM.
BUT THE TITANS ARE A GOOD TEAM. THEY PLAY OLD-SCHOOL BASEBALL. IT'LL BE A TOUGH GAME.
OH, BROTHER...

"OLD-SCHOOL"? THOSE FOSSILS ARE OUT OF DATE.
BUT THEY'RE HUGE!
Fuzzies
BELIEVE ME, WE'VE GOT NOTHING TO WORRY ABOUT.
HOW SO?
THIS GAME HAS EVOLVED, AND THEY HAVEN'T.
Fuzzies
WHAT DO YOU MEAN?
LISTEN, I'LL EXPLAIN IT.
Fuzzies

HAMMY SOSA PRESENTS THE HISTORY OF BASEBALL

Baseball was invented during the **Handlebar Moustache Era**. The balls were carved out of dried moustache wax. The players all wore top hats. Batters stood on peach baskets and base runners rode on bicycles.

Then came the **Bad Logo Era**. No one could tell what team anyone was on. These were confusing times...
YOU CANNOT TAG ME OUT, WE ARE ON THE SAME TEAM.
MY GOOD FELLOW, THAT IS AN AMPERSAND.
WHAT DID YOU CALL ME?

IS HAMMY MAKING THIS UP?
I THINK SO.
Fuzzies

Then, of course, there was the **Rubber Bat Era**, which was soon followed by the "Yo-Yo-Ball" scandal. That was a dark chapter in baseball history, but brighter days were still to come.

The Bubble Gum Era was groovy and fun and the uniforms were very colorful. Most players would like to forget the **Tube Socks Era**.

EVERY TEAM HAS ITS STRENGTHS AND WEAKNESSES.
I LIKE TO THINK THAT WE CAN LEARN SOMETHING FROM EVERY TEAM WE PLAY.
OH, BROTHER!
GOOD GRAVY! I GUARANTEE YOU THAT THERE IS NOTHING USEFUL THAT WE CAN LEARN FROM THESE RELICS. OH, I'M SURE THEY HAVE SOME CRAZY DINOSAUR STUNTS, BUT THERE IS NO WAY THAT THE TITANS HAVE ANY SKILLS THAT MODERN PLAYERS CAN MAKE USE OF!
I BET THEY DO!
IF THEY HAVE ANYTHING PRACTICAL TO TEACH US, I WILL EAT MY HAT!
THAT'S A BET!
ARE YOU GUYS DONE TALKING? THE GAME'S ABOUT TO START.
GADZOOKS! I'M PITCHING!

IT SEEMS THAT HAMMY'S LITTLE LECTURE HAS DELAYED THE START OF THE GAME.
SORRY I'M LATE!
WHAT TOOK YOU SO LONG?
YOU SHOULD TAKE THIS GAME MORE SERIOUSLY!
WHAT'S THE RUSH?
THE FIRST BATTER IS **STRUTHIE O'MIMUS**...
HEY, BLUE EYES.
WHAAAA?
THIS CAN'T BE GOOD.

FIVE PITCHES LATER... THREE BALLS AND TWO STRIKES, A FULL COUNT...
STRIKE THREE!
ARE YOU SURE THAT PITCH WAS A STRIKE? IT LOOKED LIKE A BALL TO ME... BUT WHAT DO I KNOW?
AW, SHUCKS, I THINK YOU'RE RIGHT, IT WAS A BALL, YOU CAN GO TO FIRST BASE.
YOU SHOULD TAKE THIS GAME MORE SERIOUSLY!
GULP!

CAM ARASORRUS STRIKES OUT NEXT...
STEE-RIKE THREE!
AND SO DOES **DIPLO DOCUS**...
YOU'RE OUT!

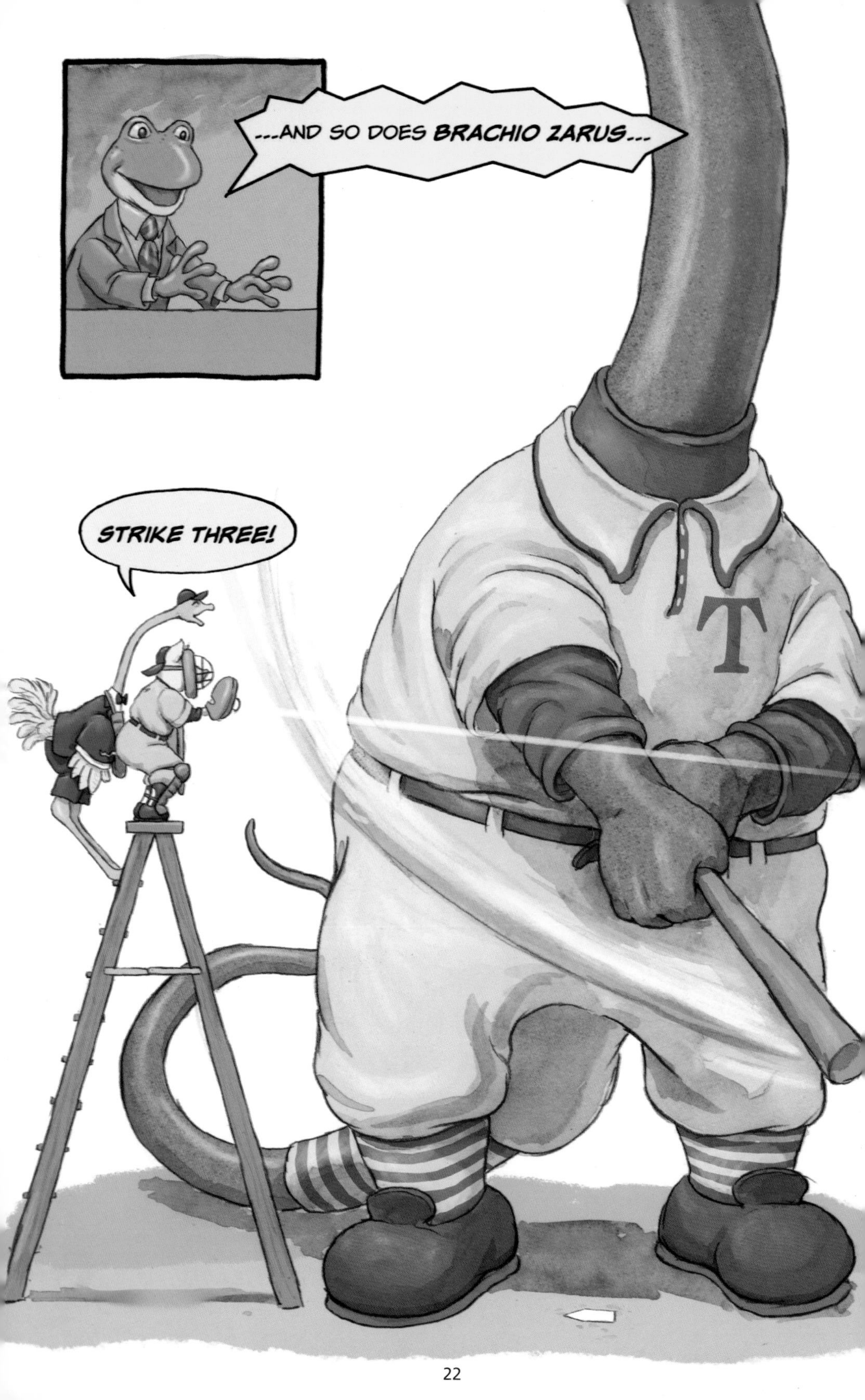
...AND SO DOES BRACHIO ZARUS...
STRIKE THREE!
T

IT'S THE BOTTOM OF THE FIRST INNING. THE FUZZIES ARE COMING IN FROM THE OUTFIELD...
IT SEEMS LIKE THOSE BIG GUYS STRIKE OUT A LOT.
THEY MUST BE GOOD AT SOMETHING...
TYRELL REX IS WARMING UP ON THE MOUND FOR THE TITANS...

PEPE PERRITO STEPS UP TO THE PLATE FOR THE FUZZIES.
ANNIE KYLO IS CATCHING FOR THE TITANS...

FUZZY FIELD
BALL STRIKE OUT AT BAT
1 2 3 4 5 6 7 8 9 R H E
VISITORS
FUZZIES
THAT BALL IS OUTTA HERE! IT'S GOING TO HIT THE SCOREBOARD!

...BUT **TERRY DACTYL** MAKES AN AMAZING CATCH!
FUZZY
BALL
FUZZIES

PAM KNOCKS IT DEEP, BUT **DONNA PTERRA** MAKES THE GRAB!
...AND **RAMFO RINKUS** ROBS **JACKIE** OF A HOME RUN. THREE OUTS, NO SCORE.
QUEI DINOSAURI HANNO TALENTO!*
PRETTY IMPRESSIVE SKILLS!
DINOSAUR STUNTS! USELESS IF YOU CAN'T FLY!
*Translation: *Those dinosaurs have talent!*

PTEROSAURS AREN'T REALLY DINOSAURS.
EVERY DINOSAUR KIDS' BOOK HAS TO HAVE PTEROSAURS. THAT'S THE LAW!
WHY DON'T YOU THROW IN A WOOLY MAMMOTH? HOW ABOUT A GIANT GROUND SLOTH?
I'M OUTTA HERE!

WELL, THIS IS AWKWARD... YOU SHOULD PROBABLY SWITCH BACK TO THE GAME.

A SWING AND A MISS! ONE OUT!
STRIKE THREE!

IT'S THE TOP OF THE SECOND INNING, ONE OUT. TERRY DACTYL IS UP, BUT SANDY LOOKS A LITTLE CONFUSED OUT THERE ON THE MOUND.
Fuzzies
THE STRIKE ZONE IS SUPPOSED TO BE BETWEEN THE KNEES AND THE CHEST, BUT IN THIS CASE...
JUST AIM FOR MY GLOVE.
Fuzzies
Fuzzies

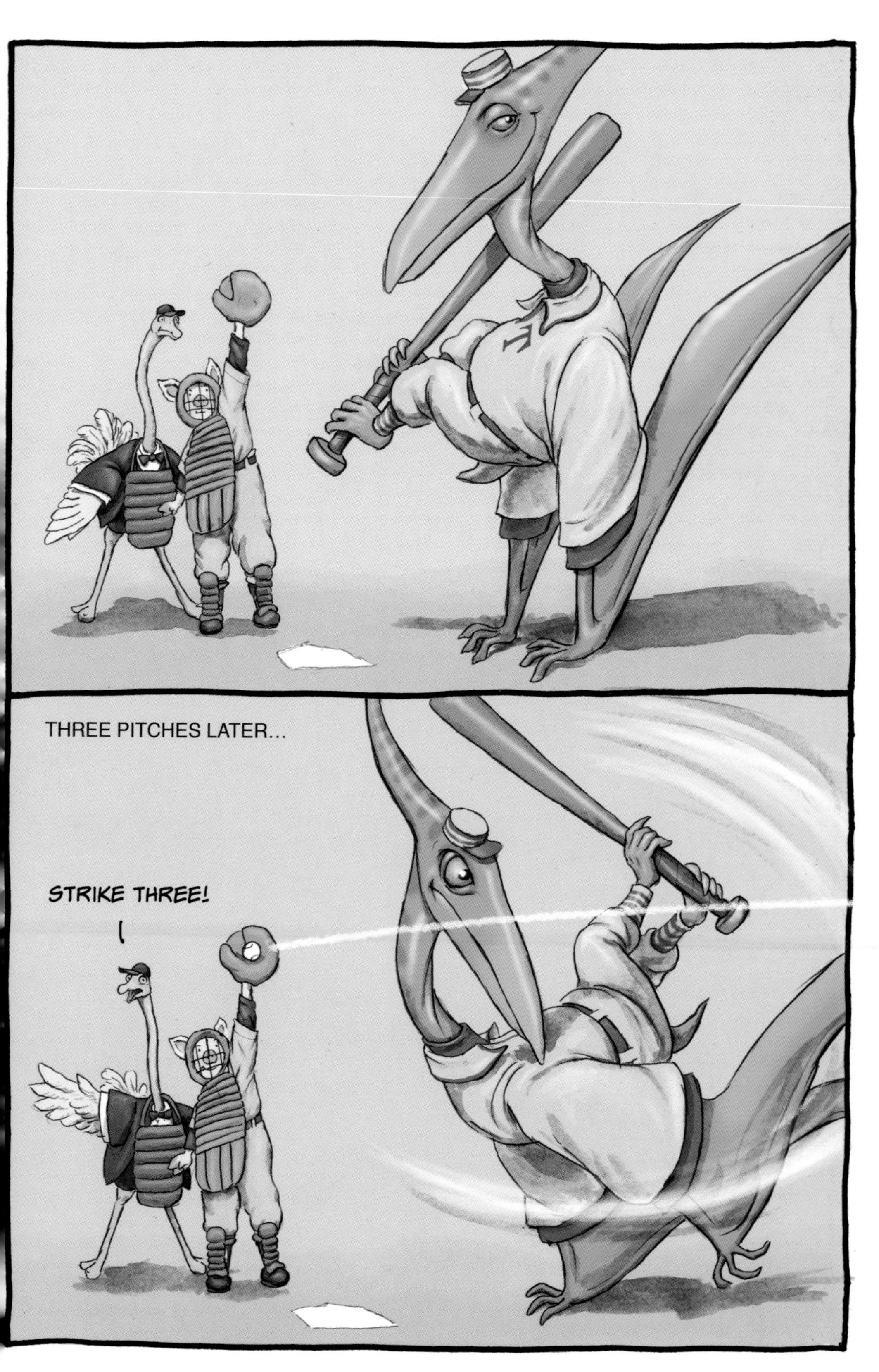
THREE PITCHES LATER…
STRIKE THREE!

THE NEXT BATTER IS
ANNIE KYLO...
FOUR PITCHES LATER
IT'S 2 BALLS AND 2 STRIKES...
STRIKE TWO!

HERE'S THE FIFTH PITCH… AND ANNIE KNOCKS IT INTO CENTER FIELD FOR A SINGLE.

EXCUSE ME, MR UMPIRE, UNLESS I'M MISTAKEN, THAT PLAYER JUST HIT THE BALL WITH HER TAIL.
YES...
CORRECT.
SINCE HER TAIL IS A BODY PART, TECHNICALLY, SHE WAS HIT BY THE PITCH. THAT CAN'T BE A SINGLE.
TRUE, BUT ANY PLAYER HIT BY A PITCH AUTOMATICALLY GOES TO FIRST BASE, SO SAME RESULT.
NORMALLY YES, BUT IF THE BODY PART IS HIT WITHIN THE STRIKE ZONE, IT COUNTS AS A STRIKE.
BUT, WAS HER TAIL EVEN IN THE STRIKE ZONE?
IT WAS! STRIKE THREE, SHE'S OUT!

I CAN'T TAKE ALL THIS ARGUING!
OSTRICHES DO NOT BURY THEIR HEADS IN THE SAND! THAT IS A COMPLETE MYTH.
ALL OF THE OTHER UMPS LET ANNIE HIT THE BALL WITH HER TAIL... BUT NONE OF THEM HAVE PRETTY BLUE EYES LIKE YOU DO!
OH, BROTHER.
AW, SHUCKS, SHE CAN STAY AT FIRST.

THE NEXT BATTER IS TYRELL REX, WHO STRIKES OUT TO END THE TOP OF THE SECOND INNING...
STEE-RIKE THREE! YOU'RE OUT!
REX
7
OSA
21
BO GRIZZLY IS UP NEXT FOR THE FUZZIES...
OKAY, LET'S KEEP THE BALLS ON THE GROUND, SO THOSE FLYING TITANS CAN'T CATCH THEM.
Fuzzies
Fuzzies

THE GRIZ HITS A SIZZLING GROUNDER RIGHT PAST THE PITCHER, RIGHT TOWARD BRACHIO AT SECOND BASE.

BRACHIO DIVES ONTO THE GROUND TO BLOCK THE BALL...
ZAF

...AND SHORTSTOP STRUTHIE JUMPS OVER HIM TO GRAB THE BAL
REX

AND THROW IT TO FIRST FOR THE OUT...
GRIZZLY
34

LARRY BOA HITS A GROUNDER, BRACHIO BLOCKS IT, STRUTHIE THROWS IT TO FIRST. TWO OUTS...
PRETTY IMPRESSIVE FIELDING, IF YOU ASK ME.
ACTING LIKE A BRICK WALL IS ***NOT*** A BASEBALL SKILL!
IF WE HIT A GROUNDER THE BIG GUYS STOP IT, IF WE POP IT INTO THE OUTFIELD, THE FLYING GUYS GET IT. ANY BRIGHT IDEAS?
NONE OF THE INFIELDERS ARE FAST, EXCEPT FOR THE SHORTSTOP. SO LET'S BUNT IT DOWN THE BASELINE.

HAMMY SQUARES UP AND LAYS DOWN A PERFECT BUNT...
PLINK
SAFE AT FIRST!
TWO OUTS, RUNNER ON FIRST, BLOSSOM IS UP...
3 HAMMY RUNS TO SECOND BASE.
1. BLOSSOM BUNTS IT DOWN THE THIRD BASE LINE.
2. DIPLO'S THROW FROM THIRD IS NOT IN TIME. BLOSSOM IS SAFE AT FIRST.
KYLO
4

CAP'N SPIKE TOPPS IS COMING OUT OF THE DUGOUT TO MAKE A CHANGE. HE'S TAKING DIPLO, BRACHIO, AND CAM OUT OF THE GAME AND SENDING IN **COMPO NATHUS**, **MASIA K. SAURUS,** AND **VINNY RAPTO**...

KAZUKI KOALA BUNTS IT TOWARDS THIRD, BUT MASIA GRABS IT...

...AND WHIPS IT TO COMPO AT FIRST TO END THE SECOND INNING.

IT'S THE TOP OF THE THIRD INNING AND…
STOP EVERYTHING! THIS CANNOT CONTINUE! THIS IS ALL TERRIBLY, TERRIBLY WRONG!

WHAT'S ALL WRONG? A PTERODACTYL CATCHING A BALL WITH ITS FEET?
A T-REX PITCHING WITH TINY ARMS?
A SNAKE SWINGING A BASEBALL BAT?
NO! THE PROBLEM IS THAT DINOSAURS HAD FEATHERS! ALL SCIENTISTS AGREE!
COMPSOGNATHUS HAD FEATHERS!
I LIKE IT!

VELOCIRAPTORS HAD FEATHERS!
EVEN T-REX HAD FEATHERS!
PROFESSOR, YOU CAN'T DO THIS! I TOLD YOU, THIS IS FICTION! THIS IS MY BOOK! THESE ARE MY CHARACTERS!
WATCH YOUR STEP, MISTER! ALL I HAVE TO DO IS SNAP MY FINGERS AND LIBRARIANS ALL ACROSS THE COUNTRY WILL YANK THIS BOOK OFF THE SHELVES!

CHOMP
TYRELL, I APPRECIATE THE THOUGHT, BUT I'M TRYING TO KEEP THIS SERIES NON-VIOLENT. CAN YOU SPIT HIM OUT, PLEASE?

I LOOK RIDICULOUS.
THANK YOU!
PLOP
PROFESSOR, YOU REALLY NEED TO FIND A DIFFERENT BOOK. STICK TO NON-FICTION.
MAY I KEEP MY FEATHERS?
I GOTTA GET A DIFFERENT BOOK.

WE'VE ONLY GOTTEN THROUGH TWO INNINGS AND WE'RE ALMOST TO THE END OF THE BOOK, SO LET'S JUMP AHEAD TO THE TOP OF THE NINTH. THE SCORE IS STILL ZERO TO ZERO, THERE'S ONE OUT, AND THE TITANS HAVE RUNNERS ON FIRST AND THIRD.
1. THE PITCHER THROWS THE PITCH, AND THE RUNNER ON FIRST TRIES TO STEAL SECOND...
2. THE CATCHER, SEES THE BASE RUNNER...
ONE OUT, RUNNERS ON FIRST AND THIRD.

3. THE CATCHER THROWS THE BALL TO SECOND...
4. THE BASE RUNNER ON THIRD RUNS FOR HOME...
5. THE SECOND BASEMAN CATCHES IT AND THROWS IT HOME...
6. THE THROW IS NOT IN TIME. COMPO NATHUS SCORES FROM THIRD BASE...
SAFE!

THE TITANS SCORE A RUN...
DID YOU GUYS PLAN THAT? HE RAN SO I WOULD THROW THE BALL, AND THEN YOU RAN HOME?
WE CALL THAT THE DELAYED DOUBLE STEAL!
MASIA K. SAURUS HITS INTO A DOUBLE PLAY TO END THE TOP OF THE NINTH INNING. THE TITANS ARE WINNING ONE TO NOTHING...
SAURUS
12
IT'S THE BOTTOM OF THE NINTH INNING. BUMP ROKHEDD IS PITCHING FOR THE TITANS AND LARRY BOA IS UP. THE FUZZIES NEED ONE RUN TO TIE, TWO RUNS TO WIN.

HEY, BLOSSOM, I HAVE A PLAN. IF I GET ON THIRD BASE, AND YOU GET ON FIRST, I WANT YOU TO STEAL SECOND. WHEN THE CATCHER THROWS TO SECOND, I'LL STEAL HOME. I CALL IT THE DELAYED DOUBLE STEAL!
WHAT A GREAT IDEA! BUT I FEEL LIKE I'VE SEEN THAT BEFORE...
OH, YES, I REMEMBER... THE TITANS JUST DID THAT TWO PAGES AGO!
OKAY, I ADMIT IT, I LEARNED IT FROM THE TITANS! BUT IT'S A GOOD PLAY, LET'S TRY IT OUT!

WE'RE GOING TO SKIP AHEAD A LITTLE BIT. LARRY STRUCK OUT, THEN HAMMY GOT A DOUBLE. BLOSSOM HIT A SINGLE AND HAMMY RAN TO THIRD. KAZUKI KOALA IS UP AND THE COUNT IS TWO BALLS AND TWO STRIKES...
1. THE PITCHER THROWS THE PITCH, AND BLOSSOM TRIES TO STEAL SECOND BASE...
ONE OUT, RUNNERS ON FIRST AND THIRD.
KYLO
4
2. THE CATCHER SEES BLOSSOM RUNNING...

4. HAMMY, ON THIRD BASE, RUNS FOR HOME...
3. THE CATCHER THROWS TO SECOND...
KYLO
4
5. BUT THE CATCHER'S THROW IS TO THE PITCHER, **NOT** TO SECOND...
T
T

BUMP THROWS THE BALL RIGHT BACK TO ANNIE, WHO TAGS HAMMY FOR THE SECOND OUT.
WHAAA?
T
Fuzzies

YOU THREW THE BALL TO THE PITCHER INSTEAD OF SECOND BASE! DID YOU PLAN THAT?
WE CALL THAT THE DEFENSE AGAINST THE DELAYED DOUBLE STEAL.
TWO OUTS, RUNNER ON SECOND
IT'S THE BOTTOM OF THE NINTH INNING. THE FUZZIES ARE LOSING ONE TO NOTHING. KAZUKI KOALA IS BATTING, THE COUNT IS THREE BALLS AND TWO STRIKES…
HERE'S WHERE I SAVE THE DAY!
STRIKE THREE! YOU'RE OUT!

THE TITANS WIN! THEY BEAT THE FUZZIES ONE TO NOTHING. THIS IS IZZY LIZARDO, SIGNING OFF!
HEY, THIS IS *OUR* SERIES... WE'RE NOT SUPPOSED TO LOSE!
TUTTI PERDONO A VOLTE.*
*Translation: *Everyone loses sometimes.*

WEEEEEEE!
MAY I SHOW YOU AROUND FERNWOOD VALLEY?
IT'S A DATE!
A BET'S A BET!

PROFESSOR DeTERRIER'S GUIDE TO DINOSAURS AND PTEROSAURS

The author claims that this book is fiction, and yet, all of the Titans are based on actual dinosaurs (or pterosaurs). His depiction of them is highly inaccurate, and the silly names are ridiculous, but the following information will show the actual creatures that the characters were based on.

Brachio Zarus is a Brachiosaurus, 66 feet long, and 30 feet high.

Bump Rokhedd is a Pachycephalosaurus, 15 feet long.

Cam Arasorrus is a Camarasaurus, 55 feet long (apparently, Cam is a miniature version).

Diplo Docus is a Diplodocus, 80 feet long

Pterosaurs are not dinosaurs, they are their own order of flying reptiles.

WATCH OUT FOR PAPERCUTZ™

Welcome to the fourth fun-filled FUZZY BASEBALL graphic novel by John Steven Gurney, entitled "Di-No Hitters," from Papercutz, those Fernwoord Valley season ticket-holders dedicated to publishing great graphic novels for all ages. I'm Jim Salicrup, Editor-in-Chief and Concession Stand Operator, here to tell you about other Papercutz graphic novel series filled with dinosaurs, who don't participate in America's Favorite Pastime.

Yes, when it comes to graphic novels about dinosaurs (not to mention girls, cats, mice, and Smurfs), Papercutz is your go-to comics publisher. First we published DINOSAURS by Arnaud Plumeri, writer, and Bloz, artist. DINOSAURS is a graphic novel series in which the dinosaurs speak and offer up factual information about themselves as they engage in comical misadventures. While the speaking and comical misadventures are fictitious, the facts are real, taken from the latest knowledge available about these creatures. Papercutz proudly published four regular DINOSAURS graphic novels and one special graphic novel in 3-D.

Currently, Papercutz is also publishing DINOSAUR EXPLORERS by Slaium and Albbie, writers, and Air Team, art. Like DINOSAURS, DINOSAUR EXPLORERS mixes fact with fiction. The series is about Dr. Da Vinci, his assistant Diana, and four kids—Sean, Stone, Rain, and Emily—and a tiny robot, Starz, who all get flung way back in time via a Particle Transmitter. Unavailable at any store, a Particle Transmitter, is one of Dr. Da Vinci's inventions that while able to transport them to prehistoric times, is only able to come back through time so many centuries per trip. As a result, Doc and the gang are experiencing every age of the dinosaurs (and even a couple ages before then!) as they travel back to the present. Each action-packed volume alternates chapters featuring the adventures of the DINOSAUR EXPLORERS with fact-filled articles about the real-life dinosaurs they encounter. Be sure to pay close attention when reading this particular Papercutz graphic novel series, because there's literally a quiz at the end of each volume. At the end of this Fuzzy Baseball graphic novel, however, is a preview of DINOSAUR EXPLORERS #3 for you to enjoy.

Another graphic novel from Papercutz, called MANOSAURS, goes in a similar, yet opposite direction from DINOSAUR EXPLORERS. While DINOSAUR EXPLORERS inadvertently travel back (then forward) through time, MANOSAURS is set in the present, and involves Leo "Doc" Jeffries, who is down on his luck with his run-down Dynamic Dino Display museum until he unearths a box of what he believes are dinosaur eggs. The eggs hatch four talking dinosaurs that rapidly adapt to their new environment, turning into human/dinosaur hybrids named Tri, Rex, Ptor, and Pterry (No relation to Papercutz publisher Terry Nantier!). While obviously MANOSAURS is a humorous, sci-fi, adventure series, it actually does explore real questions and theories such as where do dinosaurs come from? MANOSAURS #1 "Walk Like a Manosaur" by Stefan Petrucha, writer, and Yellowhale, artists, is based on a concept by Stuart Fischer, is available from booksellers everywhere.

I could go on and on. GERONIMO STILTON, the editor-in-chief of the Rodent's Gazette has gone back in time a couple of times. Once in GERONIMO STILTON #5 "The Great Ice Age," and, yeah, we know those weren't dinosaurs he met. And then in GERONIMO STILTON #7 "Dinosaurs in Action," but those indeed were dinos! (Those two graphic novels can also be found in GERONIMO STILTON 3 IN 1 #2 and #3, respectively.) And for a completely unrealistic take on dinosaurs, check out LOLA'S SUPER CLUB, by Christine Beigel, writer, and Pierre Fouillet. Little Lola daydreams about battling big bad super-villains aided by her toy-dinosaur-come-to-life James. But we think you get the idea.

Let's see, the Fernwood Valley Fuzzies have now faced the Rocky Ridge Red Claws (in FUZZY BASEBALL #1), the Sashimi City Ninjas (in #2), The Geartown Clankees (in #3), and the Triassic Park Titans—who could they possibly face next? There's just one way to find out: don't miss FUZZY BASEBALL #5!

Thanks,

Jim

STAY IN TOUCH!

EMAIL:	salicrup@papercutz.com
WEB:	papercutz.com
TWITTER:	@papercutzgn
INSTAGRAM:	@papercutzgn
FACEBOOK:	PAPERCUTZGRAPHICNOVELS
REGULAR MAIL:	Papercutz, 160 Broadway, Suite 700, East Wing, New York, NY 10038

Go to papercutz.com and sign up for the free Papercutz e-newsletter!

Special preview of DINOSAUR EXPLORERS #3 “Playing in the Permian”...

MOVE IT! THEY'RE HEADED RIGHT FOR US!
What are those?!
THEY'RE CALLED ELGINIA! QUICK, INTO THOSE TREES!
RUMBLE
RUMBLE
THOOM
Just in time...

THEY'RE BEING CHASED! BY A--
AHA!
LOOKS LIKE A DIMETRODON IS HUNTING THEM!
GREEEAH!
CRAAAH!

Fuzzies